STECK-VAUGHN

PAIR-IT BOOKS™

A Walk in the Rain

Written by Sarah Vazquez
Illustrated by Gail Hicks

STECK-VAUGHN
COMPANY

A Division of Harcourt Brace & Company

It is raining outside.

The grass is wet.

3

The swing is wet.

The sidewalk is wet.

The mailbox is wet.

The street is wet.

But I am dry!